A LETTER FOR LEO

SERGIO RUZZIER

Clarion Books | Houghton Mifflin Harcourt

Boston | New York

To Daniela, Alberto, and Cristian

Clarion Books
215 Park Avenue South
New York, New York 10003

Copyright © 2014 by Sergio Ruzzier

All rights reserved. For information about permission
to reproduce selections from this book, write to Permissions,
Houghton Mifflin Harcourt Publishing Company,
215 Park Avenue South, New York, New York 10003.

Clarion Books is an imprint of Houghton Mifflin Harcourt
Publishing Company.

www.hmhco.com

The text was set in 18 pt. Triplex Serif Light.

Library of Congress Cataloging-in-Publication Data
Ruzzier, Sergio, author, illustrator.
A letter for Leo / by Sergio Ruzzier.
pages cm
Summary: When Leo, a mailman, rescues a young bird that was
separated from his flock, the two become friends and Leo's dream
of one day receiving a letter of his own may finally come true.
ISBN 978-0-544-22360-8 (hardcover)
[1. Letter carriers—Fiction. 2. Weasels—Fiction. 3. Birds—Fiction.
4. Friendship—Fiction. 5. Letters—Fiction.] I. Title.
PZ7.R9475Let 2014
[E]—dc23
2013034502

Manufactured in China.
SCP 10 9 8 7 6 5 4 3 2 1
4500483933

Leo is the mailman of a little old town.

He carries all kinds of mail: big boxes, small packets, envelopes of every size, catalogs, love letters, birthday cards. . . .

Often, he stops to play a game of bocce with his friends . . .

or sits down for a moment to rest and chat.

Leo has a pleasant life, except for one thing.
With all the mail that he delivers every day, he has
never received a letter himself.

"Maybe tomorrow," he sighs.

One morning, Leo is about to open the mailbox when he hears:

What could that be? he wonders.

"Who are you?"
"Cheep!"
"Where do you come from, Cheep?"
"Cheep!"

"You must have lost touch with your flock, and you are too little to fly south by yourself."

Leo gives Cheep some sun-dried crickets he always keeps in his satchel for emergencies. "What should I do with you?"

"I guess I'll take you home with me. . . .

I hope you'll be comfortable here."

Time goes by.

Leo and Cheep are now a little family.

"Cheep?" says Cheep.
"Yes," says Leo. "That's snow."

When springtime comes, the birds leave their warm
winter homes and fly north.

Cheep is a big little bird now, and he is ready to go.

"Cheep," says Cheep.
"Cheep," says Leo.

Leo goes back to his life as it was before Cheep.

But what he was hoping for . . .

has finally arrived.

Cheep,
Cheep cheep cheep,
cheep cheep cheep cheep.
    —Cheep